Cooking Up a Demon

A Ghostlight Falls Story

Sabrina Cross

To the group chats -
Thanks for always being unhinged

Author's Note

This is a monster romance. Humans will be getting it on with literal monsters. Don't worry, everyone is gleefully consenting.

If you read the last three sentences and think that's not for you, that's okay. There is still time to put this book down and walk away. No one will blame you. It's the sane thing to do.

But if you're going to stick around please be aware of the following: Graphic depictions of sexual acts, swearing, depictions of shitty parents, mentions of past cheating (not between main characters)

If you feel I am missing anything please reach out to me at authorsabrinacross@gmail.com and let me know. A complete list can be found at www.sabrinacross.com

Ghostlight Falls
Dreadwither Forest
Wonder-hole
Ratcliff's
(original location) Sheet-y Stationery
Grim's Bakery
For the Plot Books & More
Kyle's
Post Office
Rosa's Dulceria
Mechanic
Ghostlight Falls Wonder Balls
Ghostlight Falls Park
Ruff & Tumble Pet Store
Ghostlight Falls School
To Fort Pines
Map
Visitors' Bureau
Skating Rink
Ghostlight Falls Performing Arts Center
Red Eye Pies
Frankie's Grocery
Ghostlight Falls Review
Ghostlight Falls Drive In Theater
MUSEUM
Carl's Adult Emporium
Bertram's Tree
Birds of a Feather Chicken Rescue
Ghostlight Lake

Chapter One

One

The bipolar weather in Ghostlight Falls, Oregon, is going to be the death of me. My headstone will read: Here lies Bea, the idiot who moved from sunny Florida to Oregon without so much as a winter coat to her name.

Okay, probably not. That is way too wordy for a headstone. But my head and nose are stuffed, my lungs ache, and the rainy weather that has persisted since my arrival in the small town two weeks ago has broken me at last.

I sneeze into my elbow before I return my attention to the recipe book in front of me. It is an old journal full of recipes in my Nonna's careful handwriting. Just reading it is a bittersweet ache.

"Five cloves garlic." I wrinkle my nose. That is a lot of garlic. But I am trusting the process with my Nonna's "Fix Shit" soup. The page is filled with adjustments to the recipe, notes in the margins. Even a few splashes, proving it was a favorite. Hell, maybe it will actually help me feel good enough to fix some shit.

"Trusting you, Nonna." I say to the empty kitchen. I dump the roughly chopped garlic in and move to peeling large carrots. The recipe is specific about them being large carrots, not baby carrots. The recipe is oddly specific about a lot of things.

The soup is at a slow simmer by the time I finish peeling, slicing, chopping, and measuring all of the ingredients. I am kind of wishing I just bought the chicken noodle from the grocery store instead of deciding to make it from scratch.

"Okay, a pinch of pepper and we're done." I find the container in the haphazardly organized cabinet beside the stove and grab a pinch. The second I drop it into the pot, it starts to smoke.

Not a little steam, but a billow of white smoke that quickly fills the small kitchen.

"Oh shit, oh shit, oh shit." I wave at the smoke over the pot as I desperately try to remember where Nonna kept the fire extinguisher. I rush to the sink and push open the windows over it before grabbing a cloth to wave the smoke toward the opening.

"You dare summon me again?" A booming voice says from behind me. I whirl around to see a creature of nightmares standing beside the stove.

It is stony grey and giant, with huge curving horns. Its horns scrape the ceiling of the kitchen, and booted feet smudge the freshly washed tile floor with some sort of black soot.

"Are you fucking kidding me?" I yell, at my breaking point. I spent two weeks cleaning up the chaos left in the wake of Nonna's death. Sure, I probably should be more concerned about the giant demon in the kitchen but...the mess!

"Who are you?" His voice a growl this time, instead of the echoing boom from before. "Where is May?"

"Dead." I say bluntly. "She had a heart attack a few months ago."

The demon seems to shrink into himself a little bit. His horns stop scraping the paint off the ceiling. Fuck. There are furrows dug into the board. Before I can yell at him, he expands back to his overwhelming size and bellows at me again.

"Why have you summoned me?"

"Dude, I was just trying to make some soup." I breathe in some of the smoke still lingering around the room. It sets off a coughing fit. I grip the side of the sink and bend at the waist as my lungs try to make their way out of my body in wracking coughs.

"Soup?" He glances at the now-empty pot on the stove.

Empty. Pot.

"Where the fuck did my dinner go?" I toss the towel over the side of the sink and move to the stove. Sure enough, the pot is completely empty. The fuck?

"Dinner?" The demon's voice is horrified. "You couldn't possibly have been planning to eat the summoning potion."

"Summoning potion? It's soup!" I turn off the burner and point to the "Fix Shit Soup" page in Nonna's recipe book.

The demon squints at the page before he throws back his head laughing. The movement digs long furrows into the ceiling. I clench my teeth against the damage.

Should I be concerned about the demon in my kitchen? Probably. But I am sick, exhausted. In the two weeks I've been in Ghostlight Falls, I've already seen some shit. I just don't have the energy to get pressed over a demon who seems more interested in laughing at me than killing me.

"Your grandmother is a riot." The demon brushes tears from his eyes before he settles his gaze on me. "What is your bidding?"

"Bidding?" I have no bidding. I don't have time for bidding. I have a store costing me money every day it's closed, a chest cold, and a demon standing in my kitchen. I am at capacity.

"You summoned me. I cannot leave until I meet the terms of the agreement. So what is it I can do for you? Revenge on a lover is popular."

I snort out a laugh. I haven't had a lover in nearly a year. Especially not since moving to the Pacific Northwest after inheriting a failing bookstore and a creaking cabin.

"No lover." He looks me over slowly with a toothy grin. A forked tongue comes out to sweep across his lower lip before blunt teeth bite into the flesh. "I could help you with that."

"No." I shake my head, sending my pink hair flopping everywhere in the loose, messy bun it's tied up in. "No, thank you. I don't have time for a lover. Unless you plan on picking up a broom I have no use for you. Be gone, demon."

"As you wish." The demon disappears from the kitchen in another billowing plume of smoke. I cough until it feels like my ribs are cracking. When I can finally open my eyes, the demon is gone.

"Well, that was weird." I pull the window closed and grab a can of chicken noodle from the cupboard.

Chapter Two

Two

I feel marginally better the next morning as I make my way into town. My head is less stuffy, and I'm coughing up mucus, which makes me feel a lot less like I am drowning. It is disgusting, but I'll take it.

After parking in the alley behind the bookstore, I head around the building to the bakery next door. The baker has an unfortunate skin condition that makes him look greenish, but he makes the best damn cinnamon rolls I'd ever tasted.

After securing my sugar rush for the morning, I let myself into the bookstore. Even pushing through the door is enough to cause my shoulders to droop. There is so much work to be done.

My Nonna left the family and moved to the PNW when I was a little girl. She and Dad had a huge falling out. I've only seen her a couple of times over the course of my life. It came as a huge surprise to learn she left me everything after she'd passed away in November.

Everything being an old cabin and a failing bookstore in a small town in mid-Oregon. While everyone said her death seemed sudden, she clearly hadn't been doing well for a while. Both the house and the store are in need of deep cleaning and repairs that speak of long neglect, not only a few months of emptiness.

I've been focusing my attention on the cabin to make it livable, but I have to get the store up and running or I will go bankrupt before I even get going. I haven't done more than stick my head inside to find the accounting books, because Nonna still did her accounting in a spiral bound notebook, for fuck's sake.

I head straight to the checkout counter and set my things down. I take a fortifying drink of coffee, then grab my ipad from my bag. Time to take some notes and make a to-do list.

Pen poised in hand, I turn to inspect the damage. Except, it isn't as bad as I remember. I hadn't imagined the cobwebs hanging like a house of horrors or the solid inch of dust on the floor, but both are gone.

"What the fuck?" I say to the room at large. There is no answer. Of course there isn't. The door was locked when I came in. There is no magical cleaning fairy.

Except, there is a demon I'd told to pick up a broom.

No. Nope. That is actually insane. Except, I can't think of any other way the store magically cleaned itself. I really hope I didn't accidentally sell my soul to a demon in exchange for sweeping up.

Three hours later, I am sitting on the floor surrounded by books. There is no rhyme or reason to Nonna's ordering. There are books that have been on the shelves for years. The return window on them is long closed. I have no clue what to do with them.

I learned Nonna's lawyer had taken care of all open invoices from the store funds. Rent and utilities are paid for another three months. I have three months to turn this chaos of a store into a functioning business.

And I have to turn it into a functioning

business because I have nothing left. I quit my job and sold everything that hadn't fit into my car. I drove for four days straight across the country. My parents told me I am insane. That I should have flown out, signed the paperwork, and sold everything.

There is something about the idea of a cottage and bookstore in Oregon that appeals to me. It isn't like I really had anything going for me back in Florida. I'd been working a soul-sucking job answering phones for an insurance agent and living in a tiny apartment with two other people. My last girlfriend cheated on me with my boss. My married boss.

The chance to start over somewhere new felt like a life preserver after days of treading water in the ocean. When the lawyer contacted me with the details of Nonna's estate, including a paid off house and a profitable bookstore, I jumped.

Except, being here and seeing the state of everything is a lot more work than I imagined. I have no clue how the store was profitable. It isn't welcoming. It seems to carry a crazy array of books that don't go together. And not a single person has knocked on the door since I arrived.

Almost as if my thoughts summoned them, there is a knock on the glass door. I nearly jump out of my skin and bump into a stack of books on aliens. The woman– girl? –on the other side ignores my less than graceful moment and offers a small, careless wave.

I manage to make it to my feet without knocking everything over and step over my fairy ring of books to get to the door.

"Hi, hello, sorry, we're not open." The words come out in manic pants.

"Oh," The woman is younger than me by a few years, but she isn't the teenager I first assumed. She offers me a wan smile and takes a step back. "Sorry. Do you know when you'll be open again? I really need a book."

I almost laugh, but manage to catch the semi-panicked sound before it escapes. I don't even know where to begin sorting out the chaos of the store. Legally, I am able to operate again. I've gotten my business paperwork in order, so there is nothing stopping me from letting her in. Nothing except the store is absolute chaos.

"I doubt you'll be able to find anything, but come on in." I step back and hold the door open for her.

"Oh, wow, did a bomb go off?" She takes careful steps into the store and manages to avoid knocking over a pile of books I forgot about behind the door.

"I've been called worse." The joke falls flat between us. I close the door and flip the lock.

Probably not the brightest move with a total stranger, but she is skinny and I can probably take her. If I fight dirty. And don't have to out-run her. "So, what are you looking for?"

"Um, some local history books. I have a thing for it." Clearly not the whole story, but I'm not going to pry. I sneeze and blow my nose on a tissue from the pack I have in my pocket.

"I think they're in the back. I haven't done much more than glance back there." The woman tucks her hands in her pockets and heads toward the back of the store with a muttered thanks.

"Are you going to keep the bookstore running?" The woman calls up to me. She's in the back corner behind a shelving unit.

"That's the plan." I shout back, picking up the stack of books I knocked over. "I think so, anyway."

Honestly, I probably don't have any busi-ness running a bookstore. Or a shop of any kind. I am good at customer service, but I have zero knowledge or ability for the rest of it.

"You should," the woman says, coming back with a book in hand. "It's kind of a mess in here right now, but the town supports our shops. I get it if you don't, can't live someone else's dream, you know?"

She hands me the book and blows a bubble

with her gum and snaps it. "Plus, there ain't shit to do around here most of the time. Ms. May kept a lot of us in books."

"It's a lot, and I'm not sure I'm cut out for it." I admit. I write down the book title and price on a sticky note beside the old register and stab it on the memo spike. Something I haven't seen used since I was a kid in elementary school.

"Eh, you are or you aren't. Maybe try doing it your way and see what happens." She hands me the cash for her book, and I put it in the register. "Would love to see some new life around here."

"Thanks... I'm sorry, I didn't catch your name."

"Delia," she says as she takes her book from me. "Welcome to Ghostlight Falls..."

"Bea," I fill in for her. "Thanks. For the welcome and the pep talk."

"No problem. Just don't tell anyone. Mostly because they won't believe you. I'm not known for my pep."

And with that, Delia leaves me alone. My mind racing with possibilities and $20 in the cash drawer.

Chapter Three

Three

Rain. Again.

I knew the PNW was rainy. Of course I knew. But fuck, I am tired of the rain. And the grey. And the constant humidity frizzing my hair.

I'm determined to have a good day. My conversation with Delia motivated me, and I am going to turn the dreary old store into a place I love. First up, is moving all of the shelves away from the walls so I can scrub and paint them.

Which means removing all of the books from the shelves. Hundreds and hundreds of books. Sigh.

Instead of thinking about the task ahead, I

turn the lock behind me and carry my bags to the counter. My little haul is going to bring me happiness. I am sure of it.

I pull the hot plate out of the bag and unpack it before plugging it in. Next comes the large glass pot wrapped in paper. I sit it on the hot plate and fill it with distilled water as the recipe states.

The cutting board and knife came from home. I sit them on the counter and get to work, occasionally checking the book to make sure I am getting it right. Two apples, three oranges, and a lime all cut into slices. Fresh bay leaves and mint. I carefully pull the petals off a single yellow rose before finding a large mason jar to put the rest of the bouquet in. A sprig of rose-mary and let simmer.

I turn on the hot plate and wait for the happiness to infuse the store. I am still cleaning up the supplies when the pot begins to spew plumes of thick smoke.

"Motherfucker!" I scream at the billowing smoke. "Not again!"

"Human, there are consequences for summoning me." The large stone grey demon is back, and looks just as annoyed as the first time.

"I was making a simmer pot!" I yell at him, throwing my hands in the air. "I was not summoning anything! I couldn't if I tried."

"My presence here suggests otherwise." The demon crosses to the counter to look at the open book. He reads the page and throws back his head and laughs.

"It's not funny!" I stomp my foot. Nothing about this is funny. In fact, it should be impossible. I've seen some strange and questionable things, but demons just don't exist.

Except the proof they do stands in front of me with his hands on his hips and a glare that should stop my heart on the spot.

"What?" I snap, annoyed at not only his presence but the loss of my pot of happiness.

"Well, what task have you for me this time?" He looks around the shop with a sigh. "Please do not ask me to dust again. I was getting it out of my nose for days."

I bite my cheek to keep from laughing at the idea of this giant demon sneezing out dust balls for days. It's disgusting and ridiculous.

"I don't want anything from you. I feel like making deals with a demon is very bad for my life expectancy. So, shoo." I wave him off with my hands. "Be gone demon!"

"It doesn't work like that, human." He sighs and leans against the counter. "Look, you've summoned me, you've already paid the price for the summoning with your spell."

"There was no spell!"

"You might as well get the work," he goes on, completely ignoring me. "Your grandmother understood the price of the bargain. Did she not explain it to you?"

"Nonna didn't explain shit to me," I gripe. I wish she had left me something to explain the last few months of my life. I wish she had explained why I inherited everything instead of my father. And I am definitely curious about the demon that keeps appearing every time I try to cook out of the family recipe book.

"She set the terms, a favor for a day." He says it as though it made perfect sense. It doesn't. Nothing makes sense.

"A day?" I ask, certain I don't want the answer.

"Favors come with a price, human. I did her a favor and May gave me a day of her life. Now it's your turn. You've already paid the day by summoning me. Might as well get something from it."

I stare dumbfounded at the demon. What the fuck did he mean I paid a day by summoning him. *I hadn't summoned him! I was making a simmer pot!*

"You're telling me I lost a day off my life because I wanted some fucking soup!" I flap my arms around like a headless chicken. "Just go away! I have too much work to do here to deal with this. Go. Let me move my millions of books so I can paint the walls and just be happy. And stop showing up every time I try to cook something! I don't want you here!"

The demon gives me a look I can't quite put my finger on. It's almost like the affectionate look you give a dimwitted animal when they do something especially stupid.

"As you wish," And with another plume of smoke, he's gone.

Annoyed, I turn back to my simmer pot and turn off the hot plate. Maybe I could make it again and leave something out? That seems safe enough.

Decided, I grab my purse and keys and head back to the supermarket for more fruit.

When I return thirty minutes later with the apples, oranges, and limes needed to try my simmer pot again, the store is in total disarray. All of the books are piled in stacks in the center of the space, and all of the nearly floor to ceiling bookshelves have been moved away from the walls.

"Fucking demon!" I yell, frustrated. Yeah, okay, he saved me days of work by doing the task for me. But I do not want to keep making deals with demons. It does not bode well for the longevity of my lifespan.

There's no response, so I assume the demon has returned to wherever demons go when they're not pestering humans. Hell, probably. Though this demon seems pretty benign for the creatures of horror from the stories.

"Not thinking about it. Not thinking about it. Not thinking about it." I chant as I lock the door behind me and head back to the counter to try my pot of happiness again.

Chapter Four

Four

"For the love of god, stop!" I yell to the rain through the front window of the bookstore. It's rained every day for the last week. I'm starting to lose my mind.

April will be dryer, they said.

It'll start to warm up, they said.

I'm not sure who the 'they' are that determines these things, but they are big, fat liars. Fifty degrees is not warm. It's not. Especially not when it's paired with days of endless rain.

The weather is cold, wet, and ruining my plans.

I grumble at the grey sky some more before moving away from the door and across the store to the raised seating area at the far end. I can't help but feel a smidge of pride as I look around.

The faded yellow walls are now a light lilac color, the dark-stained bookshelves now painted a warm white. I'm not sure how I am getting them back against the wall again, but the new paint makes me happy.

The demon must have some serious strength because I can't get the floor to ceiling shelves to budge. There was a brief moment a few days ago I considered summoning him, but I came to my senses. I'll ask Delia to either help or suggest a workman the next time she stops in.

I wind my way through neatly packed boxes of books and pause to glare out the window again. Delia gave me the awesome idea of having a sidewalk sale to clear out the old books that didn't fit with my new business plan. Except it's been raining every day for a week. Fucking weather.

I trail my fingers over the freshly painted pink railing as I climb the three steps to the raised platform now sitting area. Well, it will be a sitting area. Once I get the couch and chairs assembled. It does have a fully functional and stocked tea and coffee cart already in place. I fill the electric kettle from a jug of distilled water and flick it on before dropping to dig through the selection of loose teas.

I have individually wrapped tea bags for the customers, but I found a treasure trove of loose teas in the back room. Each tin has Nonna's messy script and I keep them hidden behind the service cart for my personal use.

A tin labeled "A Bit of Sunshine" catches my eye, and I decide it's just what I need. Especially since it appears to be the only sunshine I'll be getting anytime soon. Taking the tin, I grab a diffuser shaped like a bee and my favorite yellow "you are my sunshine" mug before getting to my feet.

The tea smells of lemon verbena and joy as I pack it into the diffuser and place the little bee into the mug. The kettle clicks, and I add the hot water to the mug. I barely have time to take a single sniff of the steeping tea before the steam thickens to white smoke.

"No!" I yell at the smoke. "I don't summon you! There is no summoning! Go away and let me have my tea!"

Of course, the infuriating demon doesn't listen, and in a giant billow of smoke, he's there in all of his grey stone glory. He might have been intimidating if I wasn't so damn angry at him for ruining my moment of sunshine.

"You dare-"

"The fuck I do!" I interrupt his bellow. "I did no such thing. Why do you keep showing up here? Why? Just leave me alone!"

"You summon me, witch."

"I repeat, the fuck I do." I glare at him, which feels absolutely ridiculous given I'm all of five-five and he's got more than a foot and a half on me, without the horns.

The demon glares daggers and stomps his foot on the floor. I force myself not to take a step back. I refuse to give any ground to this deranged demon.

"Witch," the word is a guttural growl I can feel in my chest like the thump of bass in a club. It does nothing to settle my temper.

"Demon," I shout back. It's not nearly as intimidating and doesn't do the resonating thing his voice does. Which is probably why he throws back his head and laughs.

Asshole.

"Are you going to make me needle it out of you or are you going to tell me why you summoned me this time?"

"I didn't summon you!" I argue. Then I see the shelves standing in the middle of the room and deflate.

"Yes?" The demon offers me a fangy grin, and I glower.

"No one likes a smug demon," I mutter. The demon's grin only grows. "I didn't summon you. But since you're here, can you put the shelves back?"

I dig the toe of my ankle boot into the carpet and avoid the demon's gaze.

"Now was that so hard?" His tone is smooth, but I can hear the amusement under it. I'm tempted to kick him, but I don't really want to find out if he's actually made of stone. My toes can't handle it if he is.

"Just move the shelves, please." I glare at him as he grins at me. But he does what I ask and crosses the room to the floor-to-ceiling shelves. He doesn't even strain his muscles as he picks them up and moves them back against the wall.

I refuse to be impressed.

"Anything else I can do for you?" His eyes rake over me as he crosses the store and returns to my side.

I tense every muscle against the little shiver that look gives me. Nope, I refuse to be affected by a demon. Not happening.

"Tell me how to stop summoning you." I demand.

"Now where would be the fun in that?" He uses one large, clawed hand to chuck me under the chin, and then he's gone in a plume of smoke.

"Fuck."

Chapter Five

Five

I'm going to puke.

There's no way around it. The butterflies in my stomach are intent on churning everything up. I pace the store again, checking and double checking that everything is where it should be.

It is. I've been over the store a hundred times, tweaking and adjusting with every pass. My heart is racing, and my palms are sweaty.

Delia was here earlier, helping me set up the last of the sideline items and generally trying to talk me down. But she left for her job at the baseball stadium, and I am trying not to freak the fuck out.

Trying and failing.

"It's fine. It'll be fine." It doesn't feel fine.

The grand re-opening of the bookstore is in fourteen hours, and every cell in my body is screaming at me to run. That I am absolutely insane for trying this. That nobody is going to come in, and I'll spend the day sitting alone in the bookstore.

It doesn't matter that dozens of people have stopped me around town to interrogate me on when the bookstore was opening again. To comment on the name change from Ghostlight Falls Books to For the Plot, which I thought was cute. Now I can't help thinking it's incredibly stupid.

I probably shouldn't have reached out to local news networks to see if anyone would be interested in doing a story about the store to get some buzz going. No one confirmed they'd show up to the reopening and even if they did, the store would probably be empty.

Oh god, what was I doing?

I snag the bottle of tequila Delia gave me to celebrate the reopening off the counter and head into the backroom. There's a single-serve container of orange juice in the mini-fridge. I gulp down enough to give me space to add the tequila straight to the bottle.

The second I do, smoke starts forming.

"No. Not tonight. Not now. Not my tequila!" I wave my hands at the smoke, trying to dissipate it before the demon can arrive. And then cry out when my hand hits something hard.

"Witch." The demon says, grabbing my hand in his large clawed one. It doesn't hurt, but it's firm enough I know I'm not getting away either.

"Come on! You cannot tell me I summoned you with tequila and orange juice. That's ridiculous."

I yank on my hand, trying to free it from his grasp. He doesn't let go. He brushes his large thumb over my wrist, the claw scraping gently against the skin and giving me shivers. Which I ignore. And was totally from fear of him cutting me open and not because the heat and abrasiveness of his skin feels good. Absolutely not.

"You call, I come. That is the bargain, witch." He finally releases me, but the heat from his touch sears into my skin.

"Oh, for fuck's sake. My name is Bea. It's not human, it's not witch, it's Bea."

"That is an insect." He scoffs and I grind my teeth.

"It also happens to be my name. Deal with it." I flail my hands at him. "And I so did not summon you."

"I don't like it. What does it stand for?" His

brow furls and I want to growl at him. Knowing it would sound like a kitten compared to his growling abilities, I keep the sound inside.

"Beatrix." I bite out.

"Acceptable." He props his fists on his hips like he's won some battle instead of finding out my name.

"Oh, I'm so glad my name pleases you." My tone is sugary sweet, but I'm pretty sure my glare would scare a lesser being. Unfortunately, I'm dealing with a giant demon and not some spineless human who would know enough to run from me.

"My name is Kallax." He states the name proudly, as though it should mean something to me. When I don't respond, his shoulders droop a little.

"I'd say nice to meet you, Kallax. But we both know it's not. Now why are you here and how can I make you go away?" I shove my hands into the pocket of my hoodie and try not to feel bad about the way his shoulders sag.

Be so fucking serious, he's a demon who keeps showing up, stealing my food and beverages, and stealing days off my life completely unrequested. Like, I have a reason to be upset by this.

"You needed me, so I am here. I'll go away when you don't need me any longer. That is my bargain. So tell me, Beatrix, how may I serve you?"

For one insane second, heat flashes through my body as I think of all the ways someone could serve me. And then I get control of myself because this is a demon we're talking about here and under no circumstances could I be lusting after a demon. Even if he's half naked, with abs for days, and leather pants showing off an almost alarming bulge.

Instead, I think about the store and the opening the next morning and all the ways I could fail. And just like that, the butterflies are back. I didn't even realize they left.

I grab for the bottle of tequila and, since the orange juice is gone now, take a swig straight from the bottle.

"Bleh," I say, sticking out my tongue and shudder at the burn of it as it goes down. It is a decent quality tequila, but I am not one to do straight shooters.

"It's fine. Everything is fine. It's all fine." I chant, more to myself than Kallax. And then I take another swig because I'm fairly certain it is not all fine.

"Yes, you seem perfectly fine." The sarcasm drips off every syllable. I point at him with the bottom of the bottle and scowl.

"I am fine. It'll be great. It has to be." I

storm out of the back room and into the main section of the bookstore. The large, dark bookshelves that created all kinds of nooks and blind spots have been replaced with half-height shelves that give me a clear view from one end of the store to the other. Everything is light, airy, pastel, and makes me happy.

I'm happy. Perfectly happy.

Except, for these damn butterflies trying to batter their way out of my stomach.

"You seem stressed. I could help you with that." The demon, Kallax, says. He's following me out of the back room, and I can feel the heat radiating off of him at my back.

"I think I've had enough of your help. I can't believe I'm losing days off my life every time I try to make a damn drink or cup of soup."

I take another drink of my tequila and spin around to glare at the demon at my back. Unfortunately, I've done about four shots of tequila in a matter of minutes on an empty stomach, and the room keeps spinning after I stop moving.

"Woah, there," Kallax says, gripping my shoulders and holding me steady. After a moment he releases me and pries the bottle of tequila out of my hand. "I think you've had enough of this."

Seeing as I'm swaying on my feet and the room is a little unsteady yet, he's probably right. I want to argue with him. Just because I don't want to agree with him.

"You're not the boss of me. I can get drunk in my own store if I want to." I don't want to. I really, really don't want to. Why am I arguing against my own best interest?

"Of course you can, love." Kallax says as he herds me to the front of the store. "And after tomorrow, I'll let you get as drunk as you like. But tonight, you need rest."

I lean heavily against the counter as he moves around the store, making sure lights are off and doors are locked. When he wraps an arm around my waist the next time, I don't fight him. I'm drunk and exhausted, and it feels nice to lean against him.

He's warm and solid as he supports my weight. I can't help myself, I run my hand down his side and across his abs. I expected him to feel like stone, but he doesn't. Not really. And he's almost unbearably warm.

Or maybe that's the tequila talking. Either way, I give into the heavy pull of my eyelids for a moment and rest against him.

"Come on, time for bed."

I blink my eyes open and nearly stumble as my bedroom comes into focus. "What? How?"

Kallax doesn't answer my questions. He just nudges me toward the bed. When I don't get in, he swoops me up and gently places me in the middle before moving down to take my boots off.

"Sleep." He tugs the blanket out from under me and tucks me under it. It's nice; to be cared for. I've forgotten.

"This doesn't count," I mumble, closing my eyes. "You can't take my days."

"As you wish." There's a warm brush against my forehead and then everything goes dark as I succumb to sleep.

Chapter Six

Six

Nothing could have prepared me for the first week in business. Not even in my wildest dreams, could I have anticipated the way Ghostlight Falls turned out and turned up.

The line went halfway through town when I opened my doors for the grand reopening and they just kept coming all day long. By the time I closed my doors that first day, my shelves were nearly bare.

And it didn't slow down all weekend long.

Monday morning, I'm barely able to crawl out of bed. I planned to take the day off, but there is too much to be done. I'm making a list on my iPad while my tea steeps, bagged tea, because I don't have time to summon pesky demons, when my phone rings.

My dad's name flashes across the screen, and I grimace. He and I have never seen eye-to-eye, but, since I inherited Nonna's estate, it's only gotten worse. He insists I need to sell everything and return home, as though we have ever been the Sunday dinner family and didn't regularly go months without even speaking to each other.

I send him to voicemail and ignore the stab of guilt. Instead, I focus on the list in front of me as I add berries to my jar of overnight oats.

There isn't even time to get the spoon into the jar before it starts smoking.

"Motherfucker!" I yell. I drop my digital pencil and grab the jar of oats. I throw it out the open kitchen window.

"Well, that was rude." I spin around and there he is, in all his stony glory.

"You know what's rude? Popping up unwanted all the time. Also, wasting my food. I wanted to eat that!" I point out the window to where the now empty jar lays in the grass.

"Oh, I'm growing on you." He props his hands on the doorway and leans forward. The move shows off every lean muscle of his torso, and I can't help but trace the lines from pecs down to the string fastenings of his leather pants.

"Like a bad mold." I grumble. I go to the fridge and grab another jar of oats. After a brief hesitation, I grab one for the demon too.

The strawberries and blueberries are still on the counter by the sink, so I carry my jars there. I reach for the knife, but the demon snags it first and hip-checks me out of the way. I stumble a couple of steps before smacking into the opposite counter.

"Hey!" I cross my arms under my breasts and glare at the demon. He doesn't even look at me as he starts slicing strawberries and blueberries with a dexterity I wouldn't have believed possible if not for seeing it myself. His hands are large, his fingers broad and rough.

"This doesn't count as a task, you know. I didn't ask you to do that." The demon shrugs his massive shoulders, the muscles in his back flexing with the movement and drawing my attention. Fuck, why was it hot?

I watch with a glare as he finishes the berries and adds them to the jars. He grabs a spoon from the drawer and hands me the jars.

"Easy enough for me to do. And I'm the one who cost you your breakfast." My glare deepens.

"Like you've cared about that before." I

take the jar with the spoon, but shake my head when he pushes the other jar at me. "It's for you."

His face goes completely blank, and I feel like I've made some kind of grievous error. The demon stares at the mason jar of oats and berries for what feels like forever. I'm about to take back the offer when he looks up at me.

"You made me food?"

"Technically, you made it. I just threw oats into a jar." I shrug, feeling uncomfortable with the odd weight of the moment. "You don't have to eat it."

When I reach out to take the jar, the demon jerks it away from me. He cradles it to his chest like something precious instead of what it is, a cheap and easy breakfast. I don't say anything about the weird behavior. I scoop up a spoonful of oats and berries and begin to eat my own meal.

Kallax doesn't eat. He bounces between watching me and staring down at the small jar in his large hands with something like wonder. I don't know how to react to the weirdness, so I do the only thing I can do with the weirdness of the situation. I ignore it.

"As fun as this is," I say as I finish the last of my breakfast. "Are you here for a reason? Because we both know I didn't summon you."

One of the things on my to-do list for this week, now that the store is open and things can finally settle into something resembling a routine, is demon research. I might believe the soup was a summoning potion. I could even buy the tea is a demon mix. But there is no way in Hell, pun intended, I summoned a demon with some cheap tequila and orange juice. And frankly, I am tired of losing perfectly good food and drinks to the demon.

"You need help." The demon shrugs. He still hasn't eaten his oats, but when I go to take the jar from him again, he jerks it against his chest and cradles it there.

"I mean, I have a to-do list but it's nothing I can't handle." And it's true. Sure, my list is long, but it is a busy day sort of long, not an overwhelming long. Not like things have been lately.

I look over my list: go to the bank to deposit weekend cash, organize the store to cover all of the holes, place book and sidelines orders. I need to refill the coffee cart and get in contact with the baker about doing some regular orders of cookies. I especially wanted to get some specialty cookies for the book club I intend to have running by the end of the month.

I also need to put some time in on the website. The current one is basically a landing page with little more than the store name, photo, and hours. I have zero website setup or management experience, and it is proving to be the most challenging.

"I guess I'll hang around and see what comes up." Kallax says, with a shrug.

I think about that for a long moment. How would I explain the giant demon following me around the bakery, grocery store, the stationery shop, and the bookstore? Then I think about all of the weird things I've seen since arriving in Ghostlight Falls and realize the people of this town probably won't even blink an eye.

"Suit yourself."

Chapter Seven

Seven

Turns out, I don't have to worry about how people would react to Kallax. He opts to stay home and wash the dishes while I do the first of my errands. He promises to meet me at the bookstore by lunch with something to eat.

I remind him I didn't summon him and I didn't ask him to do those things, so he can't steal days off my life. He makes a non-committal sound but doesn't argue, so I take the win.

The grocery store is first. It's fairly empty, and I'm able to get my supplies and get out without any issue.

I try to hit up the stationery store next, but

have no luck finding it. I was certain it was by the performing arts center, but there is just an empty lot there. When I ask at the visitor center, the guy standing out front wearing giant wings tells me he hasn't seen it yet today, but he'll keep an eye out. He gives me a bright smile, and I question my life choices that brought me to asking a guy cosplaying a dragon-man for directions.

I have better luck at Grim's Bakery. I have a lovely chat with the green-tinged baker, who is happy to work with me on cookies to match the themes I've come up with for my book club. Plus, I put in a standing weekend order for a variety of cookies to be delivered to the bookstore.

Feeling satisfied, I get a mixed bag of pastries. I head next door to my bookstore. The door is locked, but the lights are on, so I assume Kallax is already there.

Instead, I look through the large windows to see the lawyer who handled Nonna's estate - a short mousy man with watery blue eyes and faded brown hair. With him is a tall, handsome man with greying light brown hair and pale green eyes. He's broad, fit, and wearing a deep, familiar scowl.

I make a mental note to change the locks on the store before pushing inside. The bell over the door rings, and both men turn to look at me. I throw my shoulders back and prepare myself for whatever this is.

"Where the hell have you been?" The tall man's scowl impossibly deepens. I bite back a sigh.

"Working." I cross to the checkout counter and place my pastry bag and purse down before turning to face the men straight on. "Hello Father."

"We've been waiting here for almost an hour, Beatrix." My dad's voice is weary, as though talking to me is the hardest thing on the planet. And for him, it might actually be. "It's a business day and you don't seem to be in business."

"I need a day off too, and the weekends are better business than Mondays are." I don't know why I'm explaining myself to him. He doesn't care.

"I don't see how you could possibly know that," his voice dripping with disdain. "From what I've heard, you've only been open for three days."

I could explain to him that I've gone through all of Nonna's books of sales history and analyzed the best and worst days. I could tell him about the many conversations I've had with other bookstore owners across the country who gave me advice on hours of operation. I could even tell him I am mostly sticking to Nonna's schedule, with some minor tweaks. None of it will matter.

"I see you've made some changes," Rodney Miller, the lawyer, says. I'm not sure if he's simply admiring the wide, bright space or trying to break the tension between me and my father. I'm about to thank him when he goes on. "It will make selling the building much easier."

"I'm sorry, what?" I can't have heard right.

"The tenant agreements may prove to be a problem, but I believe we can make a case to break the leases."

I bite back a growl. There are two small, one-bedroom apartments located over the bookstore. Both of them rented out by my grandmother and have maintained their leases since I got to town. They are lovely people, and I can't think of a single reason to break their leases.

"Hold up, I'm not selling anything." I say, propping my hands on my hips and glaring the men down. I am eye to eye with the lawyer, but Dad has about six inches of height on me. It's something he uses to intimidate me into getting his way.

Not this time.

"Don't be ridiculous, Beatrix." My father says, mirroring my position and looking down at me in the most condescending way possible. "You know nothing about what it takes to run a business. You're isolated from your family, your friends. This is absurd."

I don't bother to remind him I lost all of my so-called friends when I broke up with my girlfriend six months ago after she slept with my boss. I don't bother to remind him I quit my job because my boss slept with my girlfriend. I don't even bother to point out he's a shitty parent who I never see, even when I'm only a few miles away. And since my mother is my father's sycophant, I don't have much of a relationship with her either.

"Absurd or not, I'm here and doing it." I spread my arms wide to encompass the store with the nearly-empty shelves. It doesn't look impressive at the moment, unless you know the shelves were full three days before.

"I'm sorry, I thought this had been discussed." Mr. Miller says. "I was told you were interested in selling both the store and the house."

"You were told wrong." I keep my face impassive, even though I want to glare at them both. "I'm not going anywhere."

"Don't be foolish, Beatrix," My father snaps. "You're not qualified to do this. Do you even know the property values around here?

We'll sell the property, you can come home and stay with us until you can find a new apartment. I spoke to your employer and he's happy to take you back."

I stare at him in absolute shock. How dare he? How dare he think he can swoop in here and take my life away from me? I have worked hard for weeks to get the cabin and store into shape. And to assume I'd live with my parents and work for my cheating boss?

I want even an iota of the audacity of this man.

Before I can lay into him, the door to the back area opens. There's only one person who could be back there, and my chest goes tight at the car crash level of disaster about to occur. Before I can shout out to stop him, Kallax is dipping down to work his horns out of the storage room door.

"What the Hell?" My father takes a step toward me. I don't for one second think he means to protect me. He's absolutely prepared to throw me at the demon so he can get away.

"Hell is right, mortal." Kallax says in his incredibly deep, growling voice. The one I can feel vibrate through my entire body. "That's precisely where you are going."

My father gapes and sputters. Mr. Miller

faints dead away and crashes to the ground. None of us pay attention to the prone lawyer.

"You dare insult my mate?" My eyes fly to Kallax, and my breath freezes in my chest.

Mate? Mate?!

There is no mating happening here. There is an annoying demon who won't stop stealing my food and appearing at inconvenient times.

I scan my eyes down over his broad shoulders and torso, across the ridges of his abs, and settle on the knot of his lace fly leather pants. Okay, so maybe mating wouldn't be the worst thing, but I have a feeling mate means a lot more to him than the gutter thoughts I'm having.

"Beatrix, what is this?" My father demands. His voice is shaky, and he's not so steady on his feet at the moment. A small, terrible part of me revels in his fear. I even kind of understand it. While I've never been afraid of Kallax, he looks rather terrifying at the moment.

The red veins that blend into skin most of the time are simmering, giving him the appearance of lava under his deep charcoal skin. His black eyes are practically glowing. He's risen to his full height, which puts the points of his horns only inches from the ceiling.

I realize I might have lost the plot when the

only thought in my head about the demon facing down my father with a lawyer unconscious at my feet is that I'm going to be pissed if he scrapes the ceiling. Then again, he likes being useful, so he'd probably repair his own damage.

"You do not speak to her. You do not look at her. And after this day, you shall leave and never return."

"I'm – you can't just…" My father's face turns bright red as he babbles before trailing into silent fuming. I've never seen him speechless before, and it's kind of wonderful.

He turns to look at me again, demanding with his eyes to do something. I cross my arms under my breasts and shrug at him. He's been a crappy father, and this move is so wildly over the line. I can't imagine a world in which I will want to speak to him again.

"I can and I will. You contact her in any way, you return to this town, you cause her a moment of upset and I will drag you to Hell and tie you to the pyre myself." Kallax crosses his large arms, mirroring my position, and glares at my father. "Now go, and don't ever return."

"Beatrix," Father starts. I shake my head.

"There's nothing left to be said." I cross to the door and pull it open for him. "Goodbye, Father."

My father steps over the prone lawyer and stomps across the floor and out the door without another word. I wait until he disappears from sight before I let the door close and I slump into myself.

The silence in the store is heavy, and I don't know what to say. The demon overstepped, but I can't be mad about someone standing up for me. Especially when I am so bad at standing up for myself. A part of me is sad it's come to this, but the way my father tried to manipulate and control my life is wildly inappropriate. The fact he thought I would give into him says so much about me, and it's not an image I like.

"Are you all right?" The demon's voice is quiet. When I look up at him, the fire has gone out of his veins and he's back to a solid charcoal grey.

"I guess?" I look to the lawyer on my floor. "I need to do something about him."

The demon picks the unconscious man up and moves him outside to the sidewalk, where he drops him without ceremony or an iota of gentleness.

I hold the door open for him as he returns to the store. He waits until the door closes before he spins on me and grips my shoulders. His large hands practically swallow me up. "He is wrong. You are more than capable of doing anything you put your mind to."

"How would you know?" I look up into his black eyes and wish he had all the answers. "You know nothing about me."

The demon releases one arm and wraps a hand around the side of my neck. He uses his thumb to press my face upward until our eyes lock.

"I know enough. I know you've brought life back into this building almost entirely on your own. I've seen the changes in the house and the book store. You have a demon at your disposal and do not ask for help, but do it yourself. That kind of hard work and dedication do not get squandered. You are amazing, and you will not fail."

Tears well in my eyes at Kallax's praise. I've never been good enough for anyone in my life. I'm too plump and short to be the beauty queen daughter my mother wanted. Too average of intelligence and unmotivated to matter to my business-driven father. I've been cheated on, dumped, and found wanting by every partner I've ever had. Fired, passed over, and generally mistreated by every employer.

I can't think of a single time in my life someone thought I was good enough, capable enough. I've been questioning Nonna's choice to leave everything to me since I got the notice. A part of me has been certain I will fail and end up back in Florida with nothing. A voice I've been smothering daily.

Kallax is right. I've worked hard. My first weekend was beyond my dreams. Maybe this isn't what I planned for my life, but I feel good here. I feel good about the work I put into the store. I feel good about the people I've met and think I might even have friends here one day.

Kallax leans down until he is inches from me. His grip on the back of my neck tightens, and his expression goes fierce.

"Do you understand me, Bea? You will not fail." His voice is as firm as it was when he was sending my father away. Determined. Demanding.

I reach up and grab his wrist, holding him in place. His skin hot beneath my hand. His grip tightens even more until it borders on pain.

For a brief moment, we stand as statues. And then I give in to the feeling welling up inside of me.

I tilt my head and press my mouth to his.

Chapter Eight

Eight

Heat flashes through me the moment our lips meet. It's unlike anything I've ever felt before, and I try to pull away. Kallax doesn't let me. His grip on my neck keeps my head tilted and close. He lets out a growl, and his tongue sweeps out of his mouth to brush against the seam of my lips.

I shudder and open for him. His mouth is so hot as his tongue invades me. It's longer than human and invades deep as it twines with mine in a completely new and unfamiliar way.

He wraps his other arm around my waist and pulls me against him and up his body until my feet leave the floor. I wrap my legs around his wide torso and cling to his shoulders. I'm certain he can hold my weight, but I need to ground myself.

The kiss goes on forever until my entire body is floaty and I'm burning up with desire. His hands don't wander from his grip under my ass and on my neck, but he keeps me pressed tight against him.

My hands roam over his shoulders and down his arms. His skin is rough like leather and so warm. I'm whimpering into his mouth and desperate for more when he finally breaks the kiss.

"Not here," Kallax says as he lowers me to the ground. He holds my waist as I get my feet steady beneath me.

"Huh?" My brain is still misfiring from the kiss and the heat running through my veins. I'm not capable of words or thought.

"The door, love." Kallax reaches around me to lock the store door. "I don't mind an audience but even I'm not willing to put on a show for all of main street."

I look out the window. No one is there, but I can't believe I got so caught up I didn't even think about the fact we are in the store and anyone can see or walk in. Then I think about the fact I'm kissing a seven-foot-tall demon in full view of everyone.

"Oh, my god. What if someone sees you?" I shove him back toward the back room and out of view of the front windows. "You have to go!"

"No one in this town would blink an eye. I'm hardly the weirdest thing around here." He might be right about that. I've definitely seen some weird things since I arrived, but what if he was wrong?

"I have work to do." Kallax doesn't budge as I push him backward toward the storage room, and I plant my feet and push harder. "You're in my way. Please leave."

The demon chuckles and wraps his arms around me. He hauls me off my feet again and presses a smacking kiss to my lips before setting me back down.

"As you wish. But this isn't over." Then he releases me, and in a plume of smoke, he's gone.

I collapse against the counter and wonder what the heck I just got myself into.

***

Nearly five hours later, I let myself into Nonna's house. Despite all of the work I've put into cleaning it, it's still very much her house. I wonder if I'll ever think of it as my own.

I drop my bags onto the counter and sink onto a stool at the island. My neck and shoulders ache, and my feet are sore, but I'm satisfied with the work I accomplished. Books have been ordered, and I rearranged the ones remaining to make the shelves look a little less bare.

I'm debating a bath when my stomach growls and reminds me I haven't eaten anything but oatmeal and a pastry all day. I need food. And maybe a glass of wine. I can't decide if it's a celebratory wine or a sullen wine.

A part of me still feels bad about the finality of my father's departure, but I shove it down. I won't let his selfishness ruin my productive day. Celebratory wine and some pasta are just what the day ordered.

I put a pot on to boil before pulling a bottle of my favorite white out of the fridge and grab a wine glass. I pour myself a generous helping and take a drink. The cold, sparkling wine boosts my mood, and I decide to get a little fancy for dinner.

"Kallax, I swear to god if you poof this meal..." I grumble as I pull out the olive oil and a clove of garlic and get to work.

Thirty minutes later, I have garlic-alfredo pasta with a side of bruschetta. A part of me is disappointed when Kallax doesn't appear, despite my warning. Though I'm glad to be able to eat my meal, I miss his company.

I set the table and turn on a playlist on my music app called Whimsical Witch. It's a mix of instrumentals perfectly fitting my mood tonight. I sway along to the music as I plate my dinner.

Eating alone has never felt as lonely as it does now. Maybe it's the come down after the confrontation with my father. Or the drop after the kiss with Kallax. But I feel a little bereft.

The hum of satisfaction when I got home is gone, and a wave of sadness settles in its place. Appetite lost, I push my plate away and finish my glass of wine.

Covering my plate with foil, I pack up the leftovers before putting it in the fridge. I pour myself another glass of wine and take it to the sink to look out the window at the backyard.

The days are getting longer, but sunset is creating a stunning visual at the treeline. Brilliant pinks and oranges fade into the coming darkness. As I watch the colors fade, I have what is probably a terrible idea.

I fill the electric kettle and turn it on. Nonna has a collection of tea tins much like the ones kept at the store. I don't know what I'm looking for exactly, but I let instinct guide me. I don't even know if what I'm trying will work. I'm operating on hope.

A tin labeled 'Get Lucky' catches my eye. I

open the tin and smell the floral blend and decide it will do. I could use all the luck I can get to do something I've never imagined myself doing.

The kettle clicks off, and I grab the infuser and fill it with the loose leaves. I pick a red mug covered in hearts and set the tea to steep. I watch the water change green and hope.

"Come on, Kallax." I whisper.

When the wisps of steam turn to smoke, I jump back. My heart catches in my throat, and I second guess myself. Was this a good decision?

Too late to change my mind, the smoke increases and then there he is. The demon I haven't been able to stop thinking about all day.

"You dare summon me?" His tone is light, teasing. He leans back against the counter with his hands propped on the laminate top. It makes his biceps bulge and brings attention to his bare abs and the toned vee of his hips. When I look up to meet his eyes, his smirk says it all.

"I didn't summon you. I was just making tea." My voice is as teasing as his.

"What is your bidding? You summoned me. I cannot leave until I meet the terms of the agreement. So, what is it I can do for you? Revenge on a lover is popular."

I snort out a laugh, recalling his words as those he offered the first time we'd met.

"No lover?" Kallax looks me over with a toothy grin. "I could help you with that."

Chapter Nine

Nine

I can't hold back any longer, I step into his space. He meets me with his hands on my hips and his mouth on mine. His hands slide down to my ass until he can boost me up. He sets me on the island, and I wrap my legs around him to keep him close to me. His large hand dives into my hair, and he uses the grip to tilt my head further back and open me up to his kiss.

The demon looms over me as he plants one hand on the island to keep himself balanced as he tugs my hair and devours my mouth. I'm surrounded by him, lost in him.

A part of me is screaming 'what are you doing' at top volume, but it is so buried under lust I don't give it a second thought. If the sexy as fuck demon is down, who am I to say no?

He releases my hair to wrap his hand around the front of my neck. His thumb tilts my head up until we're eye to eye. My breath comes in pants while his is still annoyingly steady.

"Tell me what you want."

I wish I had the answer. It feels like a weighted, complicated question. Things with Kallax have shifted, not just tonight but the last few times he was here. He cares for me, defends me, and he kisses me like there's no tomorrow. But what kind of future is there with a demon who slowly takes your life, day by day, every time he appears?

I have to put aside romantic notions of something I can't have and focus on the immediate.

"I want you to fuck me," I tell him with all the confidence I can muster. For a moment, I imagine a flicker of disappointment on his face, but I have to be mistaken.

"As you wish." Kallax grips the neck of my simple t-shirt in his hands and rips it in two. I scream and slap at his hands.

"What the hell is wrong with you?"

"You want to be fucked. So I'm going to fuck you. And you're going to love every moment of it." His hands move to my jeans, but I slap them away and quickly undo the button and zipper.

"Don't you dare. Do you know how hard it is to find good jeans?" I wiggle the jeans down my hips, made awkward by sitting on the counter with a demon between my legs. "Can't you fuck me without destroying clothes?"

"It's not nearly as fun, but I suppose so." Kallax takes my jeans and I tense, but he just helps me pull them down my legs until I'm sitting on my counter in my black string bikini underwear, hot pink lace bra, and the tattered t-shirt. I shrug out of the damaged material and cast it aside with a scowl.

As soon as I'm free of the shirt, Kallax is back. His body is like a furnace as he presses against the front of me. His hand fists my hair before he devours my mouth in a kiss so intense my head spins.

I grip his shoulders and try to climb him with my legs. I want to crawl into his warmth and live there. After months of being in Oregon–with its cold, rainy weather–being pressed against him is like being home in Florida again. One of his large hands drops to my ass. His thick black nails dig into my skin in sharp points. He boosts me up until I'm gripping his horns and writhing against him as we kiss.

Kallax growls, and his grip on my ass tightens, pressing me against his torso. His other hand still tangled in my hair. I'm immobile against his large, hot body. I squeeze the base of his horns, and he bucks against me.

"Sorry," I mutter into his mouth, hoping I didn't hurt him.

"Do it again," he orders. His voice is impossibly lower, and I shudder at the sound.

I press my fingers around the base of his horns where they attach to his skull. The hard horn gives way to something that feels like the cartilage in a nose. Firm, but with some give. I squeeze there and am rewarded with another growl and his fingers gripping harder into my mostly bare ass.

I thrust against him, and he lowers me down until his cock presses between my legs, right where I need him. I grip his horns harder and wrap my legs around his tighter as he uses his grip to rub me up and down his massive bulge.

"Inside," I pant against his mouth. "I want you inside of me."

He lowers me back onto the island and uses a hand in the middle of my chest to press me back against the cool laminate top. I shiver at the cold after the intense heat of his body.

"This is the exact opposite of what I asked for," I pout. I look down my body at him. He grins and grabs the sides of my panties. "I swear I will injure you if you rip those."

The underwear aren't fancy, just cotton string bikinis. But finding panties that fit as a plus sized woman with a belly and little ass is a challenge, and there is no way I am replacing them because the demon can't take ten seconds to slide them down my legs.

"You're no fun." He curls his fingers under the thin straps and works them down my legs.

"You're not the one paying for clothes." I glare at him. "Now, will you fuck me already?"

I shift up far enough to yank my sports bra over my head. But, of course, I get stuck halfway there and growl as the stretchy material gets wrapped around my head and arms.

"Need a hand?" The demon's voice is placid, and I growl again, this time at him. When I don't reply, he reaches up and tears the fabric in two. While I want to kick him for destroying yet another article of clothing, I'm too relieved about being free. Plus, the way he tore the thick spandex like paper is fucking hot.

"Fuck, you're perfect." He growls, running those sharp nails over my skin between my breasts to the top of my mound. "I'm going to devour you."

"Stop teasing and get inside me already, damn it." I say, trying to push his hand lower. He chuckles and dips his head to press a scalding kiss to the curve of my belly just below my belly button.

"Settle, love." He kisses lower, right above my mound. "I'm a large demon and you're a small human. Some preparation is necessary."

His hands move to brace my hips, and he pins me in place just before his forked tongue comes out to lick a hot swipe up my lips from opening to mound. Because of the shape, he doesn't go near the slit or any of the places I need him the most.

"Kallax," I whine, unashamed to beg for what I need.

"Trust me, you'll love everything I do to you." Kallax says before he lowers his head and shoves his tongue between my lips to curl around my clit. The muscle presses on both sides of the swollen bud and has me bucking my hips. Which, of course, is useless with the way Kallax has me pinned to the island.

He does something—flutters his tongue somehow—to vibrate around my clit, and I yell out. I grab his horns and force his head down harder into my pussy.

"Please Kallax!" I try to thrust up against him, but his hold is too firm. The grip on his horns does nothing to get the angle or pressure I need. My entire pussy begins to tingle and I moan.

"Shhh, love. Take what I give you and you'll get what you need." He releases my hips and I buck up as his tongue resettles around my clit. His hands disappear under the counter, and I imagine him undoing the laces on his leather pants.

I want to be the one to release him. I want to see the cock that rubbed so perfectly against my pussy. I want it inside me almost as much as I want my next breath.

One arm comes back up to bar against my hips, holding me in place. I plant my feet on his shoulders and try to get an angle to encourage his tongue inside of me. He doesn't allow me the movement. I sob-growl in frustration.

"Kallax, please. I need something inside of me." The words are a sob of pleasure and frustration. I'm so close, but there's no way I'll be able to come with the empty ache of my vagina.

"As you wish."

Chapter Ten

Ten

Kallax growls the words against me before lowering his tongue from fluttering around my clit to my opening. He plunges inside with one thrust. I buck against his arm. His tongue is large and wide, and I've had penises inside of me smaller than it.

I hold on to his horns for dear life as he fucks his tongue in and out of me. His body moves as he pumps his cock below eyesight. I want to watch.

"Play with yourself. Show me how you get off." He releases me at the same time he pushes his tongue back inside. I moan and reach a hand between my splayed legs to press firmly against my clit. My middle finger presses firmly against the bundle and slides up and down. It takes almost no time before I'm riding the knife's edge of pleasure. Kallax isn't thrusting his tongue. It's vibrating deep inside me better than any vibe I've ever used. He has the forked tip pressed right against my g-spot and the direct pressure is so intense my eyes flutter shut.

Kallax lets out a little growl as my free hand slides to the base of his horn where I know it feels good. And the vibration of the sound is all it takes. I cry out as pleasure floods my body and every limb goes tense.

The pressure on my g-spot increases at the same time my finger slides faster over my clit and the tension breaks on a sob. Kallax pulls back and, to my shock, spits on my pussy before fucking his tongue back inside of me. The spasming channel starts tingling.

"What?" I ask, my voice rough.

"It's an anesthetic . It'll make it easier for you to take me." My entire pussy is tingling like a sleeping limb, and I can't decide if it's pleasure or agony.

"Coulda asked," I mumble. Before I can work up a good mad, Kallax removes my hand from his horn and rises to his full height. And I'm speechless.

His cock hovers over my body. It's impossibly long and wide. Shorter than my forearm, but not by much, I'd wager. It's bright red and practically glowing with the same lava-looking veins that came out in the shop earlier. Most interesting is the fact that under the flesh his cock almost resembles anal beads, without the string separating the beads. His cock is a fucking mountain range of bumps and valleys.

My pussy clenches and tingles, and I wonder if it would even be possible to take him. He pulls me back to the end of the island and dips his knees until the tip of his cock presses against my opening.

"Are you sure–" I start.

"It'll fit." Kallax says right before pressing in. I feel like I'm burning from the inside out as the first 'ball' of his cock presses inside of me. He's so impossibly hot, and I'm stretched so impossibly wide.

"Oh, holy fuck." I mutter, gripping the edge of the counter.

"Nothing holy about this, love." Kallax presses further, pressing another of the ridges into me. "This is all sweet, tempting sin."

There is no arguing there. I'm panting open-mouthed as he presses another ridge into me. I feel like I'm going to fly apart, and he's only about halfway in. There's no way I can take him.

"I don't think I can do it," I say. My fingers ache with the grip I have on the counter. "Too much."

"Say stop and we stop," Kallax says before pulling out entirely. I let out a whine at the instant emptiness. He grabs my hips and pulls me up. "But you can take everything I have to give you. This pretty pussy was made for me."

He cups my cunt, and I moan at the pressure against my clit and the heat of his skin. My pussy flutters, and I gasp.

"Okay, okay."

"That's my girl," Kallax says before he grips my hips and flips me over with my breasts pressed against the island. He hauls my hips up until my knees are pressed against the countertop.

Before I even have my balance back, he's there, pressing into me. The pressure is insistent as he pushes ball by ball inside of me. At this angle, he's able to press deeper, and I'm so full of him I swear I can feel the tip of his cock in the back of my throat.

"Fuck. you should see the way you take me." His hands are on my hips, pressing in, but not quite breaking the surface. Finally, finally, he stops, his hips pressed to mine.

We stay frozen there for a moment, both of our breaths coming in pants as we soak in the feel of him inside of me. I reach down and feel where we're connected. He doesn't have balls, just his cock jutting from his body. The way he's pressed inside of me has my pussy stretched to the max.

He's right, I wish I could see the way he stretches me. I make a mental note to grab my phone before next time. And then mentally slap myself for assuming there will be a next time.

Before I can spin out over the possibility I'll never feel this again, Kallax starts to move. Slow at first, letting me feel every ridge as it slides out of me and back in. I'm panting and sobbing, and it's taking all of my strength to keep myself in place on the island. My legs threaten to give out, and I kick myself for not doing this somewhere more comfortable. Like a bed.

"Fuck, love. You feel so fucking good." Kallax picks up pace, and I'm lost. His cock presses so deep inside of me, and I'm chanting a steady stream of 'oh fuck' as everything goes tight again. My muscles lock up, and I teeter on the precipice for a long moment before he slides across my g-spot just right and I fall.

He grips me around the waist as my legs give out and hauls me up against his chest. For a long moment, I'm dangling like a rag doll, too weak to even reach up to hold on to him. He drives deep one more time and roars as his cock spasms inside of me.

It's like fire in my pussy as his cum floods me. The already heated skin nearly burns with the feel of it. The unexpected and intense sensation sets off a series of aftershocks and my pussy clenches on his cock. Kallax groans and gently pulls me off him. I clench and moan with every ridge that comes free.

"Holy fuck," I pant when he's finally free of me. Followed by a more vehement 'holy fuck' as red pours from my hole.

"Oh, fuck. Oh, no. No, no, no." I reach down to touch my pussy, but while it's sore, it doesn't hurt. Not nearly as much as I'd expect for the amount of blood pouring from me.

"Hush love," Kallax says, pulling my hand free from the mess between my legs. "It's just my essence."

"You come blood?" He laughs, shaking me in his arms.

"It's not blood. It's not unlike your human male's ejaculate. Except mine will not get you with child." I blink and slap a hand to my face. I didn't even think about the possibility, and it terrifies me. What if he is wrong and I have a demon baby?

Kallax drops a kiss to the top of my head

and lowers me to my feet. My legs are shaky and weak, and I grip his arms for balance as I try to find mine. I give a shaky little laugh as I release him at last.

"You know, I've had men tell me they're going to turn my legs to jelly. I've never had anyone do it before." I grip the island and try to keep upright as my legs continue to shake. Kallax abandons me for the sink. He runs a towel under the water and returns to me. He gently spreads my legs and uses the tea towel to wash his cum off of me.

It's unbearably intimate and sweet. I nearly tell him to give me the towel, that I can do it myself, but then he presses gentle kisses to the swell of my ass and my lower back. His growl is appreciative as he moves to cleaning the pool of red cum on the floor.

"How are you?" He asks against my skin. "Did I hurt you?"

I take inventory of my body before answering. "Sore, tired, good. Really good."

His lips curve into a smile on my back. He stands to his full height, and I gasp when he scoops me up into his arms bridal style. My arms go around his neck and shoulders.

"Good, because I'm not done with you yet."

Chapter Eleven

Eleven

"Wake up, love." A grumbly voice says quietly beside my head. I wave my hand at them, unwilling and unable to open my eyes. My everything hurts, and I just want to sleep.

"I've made you tea and oats." The voice says, and I manage to crack open an eye enough to eye the demon looming over my bed. A part of me thinks I should be worried, the rest of me wants to know what it would take to get him back into my bed.

"You didn't have to do that." My voice is hoarse, and my throat is a little sore. He'd been right. Trying to suck his cock was not the greatest idea. I'd wanted to know what it would feel and taste like. But when he came in my mouth, it was like swallowing hot sauce.

He brushes a gentle hand over my head, pushing my hair out of my face. His look is tender and sweet as he cups my head and lowers for a kiss. I grab his wrist and tug, trying to pull him back on top of me.

Kallax doesn't so much as budge, of course. There is no moving a seven foot demon if he doesn't want to.

"I have to go. I'm being summoned." He presses his nose against mine. "I'll be back as soon as I can. Take care of yourself for me."

I want to tell him to ignore the summons, but for all I know Lucifer himself is summoning Kallax and he'll be obliterated if he doesn't go. I wrap a hand around the back of his head and keep him pressed to me for a moment longer before I let go and pull back.

"Come back soon." I tell him.

"As fast as possible." He promises with a kiss to my forehead. And then, in a puff of smoke, he's gone.

I think about going back to sleep, but I reach for the cup of tea on the bedside table instead. Kallax went through the trouble of making it for me, and I don't want it to go to waste. He'd gone with a strong black tea that perks me up enough to eat the overnight oats with strawberries and honey.

The sun is coming up over the trees when I crawl out of my bed and take the dishes downstairs. My legs are still a little shaky and my entire pussy is sore. It's a good ache that reminds me of all the things Kallax and I did the night before. The infernal demon worked his way under my skin, and I miss him already.

I shove it aside and wash my dishes before going back upstairs to take a shower and get ready for the day. The bookstore doesn't open until ten, but I want to go in and finish up a few things and maybe stop at Grim's for some fresh pastries. I am addicted to their baked goods.

I carry my good mood through the day. Delia comes in to keep me company as I set up the store before opening.

"You're happy today," she points out as she browses through the sports romances. "You should be. Everyone is talking about the bookstore again. It's good to have it back."

I pick up her energy drink off the shelf and move it over to the checkout counter. The open container next to my books is giving me anxiety.

"That's awesome. They pretty much cleaned me out last weekend." I want to tell her the reason I'm so happy, but I don't know how to explain Kallax to her. She seems cool and open minded, and there's a lot of weird shit in Ghostlight Falls, but fucking a demon? Pretty fucking weird.

"So, this town isn't normal," I say, testing the waters. "I'm not crazy, right?"

Delia gives me a 'well, duh' look. She pulls out a book and sets it on top of her small stack.

"Did you finally realize Grim isn't just an excessively hairy baker with a skin condition?" She rolls her eyes. "Or that stationary stores don't typically wander around."

"I knew that place moved!" I fist pump like a goober. "The guy at the visitor center was so gaslighting me the other day."

"Mappy? He probably didn't know where it ended up. I'm not sure he's smart enough to gaslight anyone. And he's definitely too nice to try it." She grabs her books and comes over to the checkout counter where I'm counting out the drawer for the day. She sets them down and grabs her energy drink.

"What makes you bring it up?" She takes a drink, and I cringe. Those things are toxic.

"I think I'm falling in love with a demon." I blurt without meaning to. I guess if you can't tell your only friend, who else is there to tell?

I didn't even know I was thinking it until the words came out. It was way too soon to even be thinking about love. Especially with a demon who pops in and out of my life on his whim. Maybe it's the orgasms talking.

"Huh," she takes another drink and shrugs. "Haven't seen one of those around here. You'll have to introduce us."

And that is that. She changes the topic to sports romances. We talk books, upcoming book club, and she fills me in on some town gossip, including the latest Ask Ali claiming the Sasquatch kids were ruining the whole town by existing. It's nice and normal and exactly what I need.

She leaves shortly after the store opens for the day. Traffic feels slow, especially after the rush of the weekend, but I do decent business for having most of my shelves cleared out.

By the time I get home that night, I'm equal parts exhausted and wired. I warm up my dinner from last night and eat it standing at the island. I'd sanitized it with bleach that morning after my shower. Flashes of last night with Kallax shudder through me.

Before I can think better of it, I put my dirty dishes in the sink and pull out the kettle. I make a cup of Getting Lucky tea while thinking of Kallax. But the tea doesn't smoke away, and the demon never appears.

Chapter Twelve

Twelve

"Thanks for coming," I tell the last of the readers who came to see the guest author, Mona Lotz, who is travelling through the area. Mona is a popular paranormal romance author, and I am lucky she reached out to me. I am also lucky Delia was willing to jump in and help with crowd control.

I lock the door and lean against it before blowing out a breath. Mona and Delia are long gone, and now the last of the readers are gone, I can get cleaned up and head home.

Not that home holds much appeal. Another night eating at the island by myself doesn't exactly sound like fun. Nor does another night reliving the single night I spent with a demon.

It has been almost a month since he left. I am tired of calling myself an idiot for still hoping with every cup of tea or pot of soup he'll appear. I'm definitely an idiot for still wanting him.

Delia has pointed out demons are kind of notorious for shitty behavior. There is something about my last moments with Kallax that eats at me. He'd been so sweet, and I believed he was coming back.

I quickly count down the drawer, store everything in the safe and head home. I know I should take care of the table and chairs and do a general cleaning, but tomorrow is Monday. I can come in on my day off. Again.

It took a little, but I've realized there is no such thing as a day off when you own your own business. I haven't taken a single one since I arrived in Ghostlight Falls.

I stop by the grocery for salt and lime before heading home. I take a moment to appreciate Nonna's gardening before I head inside. June has early flowers blooming. I can't name most of the flowers or plants, but they are pretty and bring me peace.

A peace I need before heading inside and to the kitchen where memories linger. I've been through Nonna's recipe book from front to back, and there's nothing about summoning demons in there. Everything appears to be old family recipes.

I'm after a different type of recipe tonight. I pull the tequila and Cointreau out of the cabinet. It takes no time to slice the limes and mix myself a margarita. I'm adding the agave syrup when it begins to smoke.

I drop the bottle of agave to the counter and spin around to see the demon forming. I don't even have it in me to be mad at the waste of good liquor.

As he forms and solidifies, a fine rage starts simmering under my skin. He fucked me five ways to Sunday and then left me for a month without a word. Now here he is showing up uninvited like nothing ever happened. What the actual fuck?

The smoke clears, and there he is standing and staring at me. For a long moment, we look at each other. Then he reaches for me, and I step to the side, out of his grasp.

"Oh, no you don't." I hold up my hands to ward him off. "You don't get to just materialize in here."

He cocks his head and then nods. "That's reasonable."

"Where the hell have you been?" I cross my arms over my chest and glare at him.

"Hell." He shrugs and comes to stand next to me at the counter and begins mixing a drink. "I was forbidden from coming topside."

"What? Why?"

He doesn't say anything as he finishes mixing the drink before pouring it into a heavy glass tumbler. He offers it to me.

"I broke the rules." My stomach clenches, and I set the drink I just accepted back down on the counter.

"Are you okay?" I can't imagine the punishment for breaking rules in Hell is pleasant.

"I'm fine, love." He picks up my drink and downs it in one gulp. "It took me some time and effort to make my way back."

"What did you do?" Equally, breaking rules in Hell has to be something terrible, right?

"Demons aren't allowed positive emotions. They beat them out of us in the early days. Feeling them is forbidden, forming attachments because of them is a punishable offense." He begins to mix another drink, and I think about his words.

"Positive emotions?"

"Demons feed off of people's negative emotions and sinful thoughts and deeds. We survive off deals we make with good people."

He doesn't meet my eye as he pours the drink into the glass and pushes it back to me.

This time, I drink it down. Kallax survived because of his deal with Nonna. The one he transferred to me. Our deal can't be enough to sustain him.

"So, you show up because I'm your meal ticket." It hurt to think that's all it was. Would fucking someone you were feeding off of earn him some kind of bonus? It hurts too much to think about to ask.

"No, I tried to not come. I didn't want to hurt May. I enjoyed her. But summons must be answered and if not me, then it would have been someone else. I tried to help as much as it hurt."

"And me?" I grab the bottle of tequila and take a shot straight from the bottle.

"A summons must be answered." He takes the bottle and downs half of it in one go. I snag it back before he cleans me out.

"Got it." I think about the Fix Shit Soup and Bit of Sunshine tea. How many ways had Nonna been summoning the demon? How much time had he taken?

"You don't, though." He takes the bottle from me and sets it on the counter before cupping my face in one large hand. "Someone was going to answer your call, and I wanted it to be me."

"I never called you though." He winces, and I smack him in the chest. "I never summoned you! I knew it!"

He shifts until his palm presses against my neck. He isn't gripping, but I still swallow against his hand.

"You summoned me." He tightens his grip a little, pulling me up onto his toes. He leans down until his lips press against mine. "The first time."

"And the rest?" I ask against his lips.

He takes my mouth in a bruising kiss that leaves me breathless. His hands move to cup my ass and raise me up against his body until our faces are level. I love the easy way he handles my weight. I've never been a small woman and have never had anyone able to lift me without risk of straining something. The way Kallax makes me feel small and dainty does something fuzzy to my chest.

"I couldn't keep away." Kallax says, breaking our kiss. He nuzzles into my neck and breathes me in. I grip his shoulders and push him back.

"Is that why you're in trouble?" Black eyes meet mine, and I can tell he doesn't want to tell me.

"Demons aren't allowed to feel good." He presses a kiss to my forehead. "You make me feel good."

My heart sinks. I imagine all kinds of scenarios of Kallax being hurt because of me. I think of all the ways I treated him and talked down to him when he was risking everything to be here. Realization dawns, every visit puts him at risk.

"You shouldn't be here then." I push back, trying to get him to put me down. "You should go. Don't put yourself at risk. Not for me."

"You're the first person I've wanted to risk everything for in five centuries." He holds me closer to him and shifts his grip until he's drawing my legs around his waist.

"I've seen civilizations rise and fall, kings and self-proclaimed gods die. I've seen the best and worst of society and have never wanted anything like I want to be with you."

My heart seizes. He hardly knows me, and I've mostly been terrible to him. It makes no sense he would risk everything for me.

"It's not worth your safety." My grip on his shoulders tightens. "Please, don't risk yourself."

"I'm not." When I start to shake my head, he shifts his grip again until he's boosting me with one hand and using his other hand to grip my chin. He uses his grip to force me to meet his eyes.

I blink back tears and try to resist his gaze, but his grip is firm and demanding. There's no escaping it.

"I've spent the last month calling in every favor, searching for every loophole, and bending every rule I've ever come across, but I'm here. And, if you'll have me, I'm not going anywhere."

"What do you mean? Won't you get summoned back? I can't do this again, Kallax. I can't go on not knowing where you are and if you're okay."

"Oh love, no. Not again. Never again." He presses a gentle kiss to my mouth and sets me down on the counter, but maintains his position wrapped between my legs.

He uses gentle fingers to wipe at the tears that start falling without me noticing. His gentleness has my throat tightening.

"You summoned me. Which binds us together. If we reverse the deal, we'll be able to stay together."

"What do you mean? Reverse the deal?" I try to remember the exact deal he told me, but I hadn't really been paying attention. I knew every time he showed up he stole a day off my life. Which, at thirty, isn't a big deal. It will be one day.

"Every day, you do me a favor and you take a day off my life."

"Kallax, no!" I'm horrified he would even suggest it. I don't want any of his days.

"I have a lot of days, love. And can always get more. It'll be a hundred years or more before we go through my life span. I don't want to live in a world without you in it, and this way I get to stay with you."

He pauses and takes a deep breath. "That is, assuming you want me around."

"Of course I do." I can see how he wouldn't know that. I've given him very little to believe I want him around. Sure, we fucked every which way but, before then, I'd resisted his presence. I've had time to think about how I felt about him and know the last month without him sucked. I missed his interfering presence.

"It would mean you can't have children."

"Don't want them."

"You could change your mind."

"I have an IUD and I've tried for the last decade to get a hysterectomy. It isn't changing. What else?"

His forked tongue sweeps out to dampen his lower lip, and I figure I'm really not going to like this next part.

"A favor for a day." He repeats.

"What counts as a favor? Me making you breakfast? Doing your laundry? Giving you a blowjob."

"Yes." His eyes drop to my mouth, and I flush hot as I think about the first and last time I'd had my lips wrapped around his huge cock. "That would do it."

I press my hands against his chest until he takes a step back. I slide off the counter, trapped between the cool laminate and hot demon.

"I guess you'd better let me get started then." I drop to my knees.

Chapter Thirteen

Thirteen

"Honey, I'm home." I call, letting myself into the cottage. I walk into the kitchen to find Kallax standing at the stove wearing nothing but his leather pants and a frilly white apron I'd bought him as a joke months ago.

He insists on wearing it when cooking and cleaning. I can't decide if it's because I gave it to him or because he knows it amuses me and is trying to make me laugh.

"How was work?" Kallax asks, blowing over a spoonful of red sauce. He offers the spoon to me, and I taste it. I let out a small moan as flavor explodes over my tongue.

Kallax doesn't eat. Not people food. He told me once he sips off of other's sins when he encounters them, but he doesn't drain anyone. Since people aren't dropping dead all over Ghostlight Falls, I believe him.

One of the things he's found great joy in since moving topside is cooking. I thought he was just doing it to please me at first, because he's that kind of demon, but he really seems to like doing it.

"Perfect." I say, releasing the spoon from my mouth. "Work was good. Biggest group for book club yet."

For the last few months, I've managed to grow my first book club to fifteen members. Plus, there has been enough interest to start two more for contemporary romance and mystery novels. My schedule is filled with local and visiting authors looking for places to hold book release parties or small signings. I even have a wedding booked for next month.

The satisfaction of seeing the bookstore grow is so huge I don't know how to handle it sometimes. It's nothing compared to what I feel coming home to Kallax every day.

He's everything I've ever wanted and gave up believing I could have. He doesn't mind I hate mornings and like going to bed early. He enjoys caring for me. And I enjoy caring for him.

"I ran into Kyle today." I say casually,

setting my bag on the island before jumping up to sit on the laminate top.

Kallax doesn't say anything, but turns back to the sauce, adding a pinch more salt before setting it to simmer. He reaches for a stockpot and fills it with water for the pasta.

"He says he might need an extra set of hands in the kitchen. You know, if you're interested." For weeks now, I've been trying to convince Kallax to get out of the house. As much as I love having him to myself, it's not fair of me or good for him to be stuck in my house all the time.

For the moment, I'm keeping store hours down to what I can manage on my own and don't have a need for a second seller. I have plans to expand in the winter, but I don't think Kallax will find satisfaction in selling romance novels. The demon belongs in the kitchen.

"Why are you trying to get rid of me?" Kallax asks, setting the pot on the stove to boil.

"You know I'm not." I grab his arm and tug on it until he turns around and I can drag him into my arms. "But I think you should get out more. You could do the early shifts while I'm working and we could still spend all night together."

"I'll think about it." Kallax drops a kiss to

my lips, and I wrap my arms and legs around him, holding him to me.

We stay like that, kissing until the beeper goes off to remind Kallax to add the pasta to the pot. I slide off the island and go upstairs to take a quick shower while he finishes dinner. When I come back downstairs, he's set up the small table on the deck with dinner, wine, and even lit a couple of candles.

My first thought is to ask what the occasion is, but there isn't one. Kallax just does stuff like this. He likes taking care of me, spoiling me, loving me. And I'll never get enough of it.

"I still owe you a favor," I tell him. He makes it hard to do favors for him. He prefers doing things for me. It's maddening.

"How about today, you just love me?"

"I do that every day."

"Then it should be easy."

"You're infuriating."

"And you love it."

I do.

I came to Oregon nine months ago with a broken heart looking for a fresh start. And I got everything I could have dreamed of and more. Ghostlight Falls is the weirdest town on Earth but it is the place that gave me a home, friends, and the love of my life. I never want to be anywhere else.

Check out all the stories in the Ghostlight Falls series!

The Totally Typical Tale of Mappy McMapface

Nicole Parker

Paper and Passion

Thea Masen

Romanced by the Rat

G.M. Fairy

Bread by the Grim

Dakota Cockaday

Cooking Up a Demon

Sabrina Cross

Twi-flight

Luna Cantrip

Taking a Tumble

Clover Holloway

Defined and Defiled

Elsie LePlant

About the Author

Sabrina Cross (she/her) is a neurospicy 80's baby from the middle of nowhere Michigan, where she still lives with her cat. She came into her monster romance era early when she fell in love with Beast from the 1997's X-Men animated series. After discovering sentient object romance in early 2023, Sabrina decided to embrace what she calls her 'Hold My Beer' style of writing and gave into the lifelong dream of being an author. When not writing weird monster/sentient object smut, Sabrina can be found hanging out on social media (@authorsabrinacross), reading, or hoarding office supplies.